No Bones About It

For Mandy and Ian,
great kids, no bones about it!—N.K.

To Ron and Kellie,
light box builders extraordinaire!—J&W

Text copyright © 2004 by Nancy Krulik. Illustrations copyright © 2004 by John and Wendy. All rights reserved. Published by Grosset & Dunlap, a division of Penguin Young Readers Group, 345 Hudson Street, New York, New York 10014. GROSSET & DUNLAP is a trademark of Penguin Group (USA) Inc. Printed in the U.S.A.

Library of Congress Cataloging-in-Publication Data

Krulik, Nancy E.
No bones about it / by Nancy Krulik ; illustrated by John & Wendy.
p. cm. — (Katie Kazoo, switcheroo ; 12)
Summary: Katie and her third-grade class go on a field trip to the natural history museum where Katie finds herself magically transported into the body of their tour guide.

[1. School field trips—Fiction. 2. Natural history museums—Fiction. 3. Magic—Fiction.] I. John & Wendy. II. Title.
PZ7.K944No 2004
[Fic]—dc22
III. Series: Krulik, Nancy E. Katie Kazoo, switcheroo ; 12.

2003019761

ISBN 0-448-43358-3 (pbk.)
H I J

No Bones About It

by Nancy Krulik • illustrated by John & Wendy

Grosset & Dunlap

Chapter 1

"Ouch!" Katie Carew shouted. She turned around and stared at Kevin Camilleri. "Stop kicking the seat!"

Kevin grinned at Katie. "I didn't do it. George did."

George Brennan was sitting next to Kevin on the school bus. The kids in class 3A were on their way to the Cherrydale Museum of Natural History for a field trip.

"It wasn't me," George assured Katie.

"It must have been a ghost," Kevin joked.

Katie sighed. "I don't care who it was. Just stop kicking."

As Katie turned back around in her seat,

one of her best friends, Suzanne Lock, let out a yelp.

"George, keep your disgusting hands off my ponytail!" she shouted. "It took me hours to get it right. You're going to ruin it."

"You mean you *meant* for it to look like that?" George asked.

Suzanne looked at Katie. "Boys!" she huffed. "They're all pains in the neck."

"Jeremy's not a pain," Katie pointed out.

Suzanne rolled her eyes. "He's *your* friend, Katie. Not mine."

It was true. Jeremy Fox was Katie's other best friend. But he and Suzanne did not get along at all.

Katie looked across the aisle. Jeremy was sitting next to Manny Gonzalez. They were making bunny ears over Becky Stern's head. Katie was glad Suzanne didn't see them. It would only prove her point.

"Hey, Jeremy! Manny! Watch this," George called out. He stuck his tongue out at a car that was passing by.

"How about this?" Manny said. He squashed his nose and mouth up against the bus window.

"You guys better stop that," Katie warned them. "If Mrs. Derkman catches you, you'll be in big trouble!"

"She's all the way in the front of the bus," George said. He looked out the window and stuck his tongue out again as another car drove by.

Jeremy held up a camera. "Hey, George, say cheese."

George made a funny face as Jeremy snapped a photo.

"What was that for?" George asked him.

"I'm taking pictures of our field trip for the *Class 3A Times*," Jeremy explained. He was editor of the class newspaper.

"Cool, how about this one?" George asked. He stood up and held his ears straight out as a car passed by.

"Mrs. Derkman will be really mad," Katie reminded them.

George sighed. "Katie Kazoo, you're a goodie-goodie!" he exclaimed.

"I am not!" she insisted.

"You are, too," George told her. "You never

get in trouble. You never do anything wrong. You're a goodie-goodie."

"Goodie-goodie," Kevin repeated. "Katie is a goodie-goodie."

"Katie is a goodie-goodie," Manny joined in. "Katie is a goodie-goodie."

The boys' chanting grew louder and louder. Katie's face got redder and redder. She was mad. And she was hurt, too. After all, Katie and George were friends. She'd been the first one to be nice to him when he was the new kid at school. And George was the one who had given Katie her way-cool nickname, Katie Kazoo.

But George sure wasn't treating Katie like a friend right now. He kept on singing, "Katie is a goodie-goodie, Katie is a goodie-goodie."

"That's enough!" Mrs. Derkman shouted from the front of the bus.

The boys quieted down right away.

"It's almost the end of the school year. By now, I would expect you to know how to act on a field trip. If you children cannot behave, I will ask Mr. Bloom to turn this bus around right now. We can go back to school and have a math test instead of a field trip," Mrs. Derkman warned.

Suzanne looked at Katie. "See, I told you boys were rotten!"

"George was mean. And he was wrong. I'm not a goodie-goodie," assured Katie.

"Well . . ." Suzanne said slowly. "Not all the time, anyway."

"What's that supposed to mean?" Katie asked her.

"Nothing," Suzanne said. "It's just that you hardly ever get in trouble."

"I do, too," Katie insisted.

"When?"

"There was that time Mrs. Derkman read our note out loud," Katie said. "We got in trouble then."

"That was months ago," Suzanne reminded her. "And I was the one who sent the note in the first place. You were just answering me."

"How about the time Mr. Kane caught me with a cell phone?"

Suzanne laughed. "Me again. It was *my* cell phone, remember? I brought it to school. You were just holding it when Mr. Kane walked into the cafeteria."

Katie looked across the aisle at Jeremy. "You don't think I'm a goodie-goodie, do you?"

Jeremy didn't answer.

"*Jeremy,*" Katie insisted.

"It's okay to be a goodie-goodie," Jeremy said finally. "Everybody has to be something. George is funny. Kevin is the Tomato Man. I'm good at sports . . ."

"I'm fashionable," Suzanne added. "Mandy's really smart. Zoe's an artist . . ."

"And you're a goodie-goodie," Jeremy finished. "It's just who you are."

"We like you anyway," Suzanne said.

Katie frowned. Somehow, that didn't make her feel any better.

Chapter 2

As the bus rolled along, Katie stared out the window. She tried not to think about what her friends had said. But she couldn't help it. Especially since George and Kevin kept whispering, "Goodie-goodie, goodie-goodie," into her ear.

Katie wanted to ask Mrs. Derkman to make them stop. But telling on the boys would only make her seem like more of a goodie-goodie.

The truth was, George couldn't be more wrong. Katie had actually gotten into trouble lately. Lots of trouble.

In the past few months, Katie had wound

up in the boys' locker room, started a food
fight in the cafeteria, and completely ruined
Becky's report on Cleopatra. She'd also
wrecked part of Mrs. Derkman's prized garden.
George would have loved to have seen that!

But none of Katie's friends knew about
the trouble she had gotten into.

How could they?

All those things had happened when Katie
had magically turned into someone else. But
Katie couldn't tell her friends that. They never
would believe her. Katie wouldn't believe it
either, if it hadn't happened to her.

But it really did happen. Katie Carew turned into other people . . . a lot!

It all started one day at the beginning of the school year. Katie had lost the football game for her team, ruined her favorite pair of pants, and let out a big burp in front of the whole class. It was the worst day of Katie's life. That night, Katie had wished she could be anyone but herself.

There must have been a shooting star overhead when she had made that wish, because the very next day the magic wind came and turned Katie into Speedy the class hamster! Katie had escaped from the hamster cage, and wound up in the boys' locker room, stuck inside George's stinky sneaker! Luckily, Katie had turned back into herself before George could step on her.

The magic wind came back again and again. It turned her into Lucille, the lunch lady, and Katie had started a food fight with some really gooey egg salad. The wind had turned her into other kids, too, like Jeremy and Becky. Once, the magic wind had even turned Katie into her very own dog, Pepper. That time, she'd chased a particularly nasty squirrel into Mrs. Derkman's yard—and had destroyed her teacher's favorite troll statue.

Katie never knew when the magic wind would come back again. All she knew was that when it did, she was going to wind up getting into some sort of trouble—and so would the person she'd turn into.

See? Katie wasn't a goodie-goodie at all.

Unfortunately, she was the only person who knew it.

Chapter 3

"Okay, class, follow me," Mrs. Derkman said as she walked up the stone staircase that led to the museum. "Remember, we have to be on our best behavior."

A tall, skinny man with a thin tuft of hair on his head walked over to greet the class. "Hello. You must be from Cherrydale Elementary School," he said.

"Yes, we are," Mrs. Derkman replied. "Are you the volunteer who will give us our tour?"

The man quickly shook his head, and pointed to a badge he wore on a chain around his neck. "I'm the Director of the Education Department," he said proudly. "But the volunteer who was supposed to take you around called in sick. So I got stuck . . . I mean, um . . . so I got the pleasure of giving you the tour. I'm fitting you in before my next appointment. I'm going to give a very important scientist, Dr. Franklin P. Muffinstoffer, a tour of the museum."

"Oh, well . . . that's wonderful," Mrs. Derkman said. "We're very lucky to have you as our guide."

"You certainly are," the man boasted.

"I'm Mrs. Derkman," the teacher said, holding out her hand.

"I'm Mr. Weir," the man replied, shaking her hand.

"Did you hear that?" George whispered. "His name is Mr. Weird."

"He said his name was Mr. Weir," Katie corrected George.

"I don't know," Kevin said. "He looks weird to me!"

Some of the kids giggled. Mrs. Derkman

didn't. "Children!" she scolded. "This is not how we behave in a museum."

"Oh, don't worry," Mr. Weir assured her. "I can handle a bunch of children."

Katie looked over at George. She could tell he was already planning something bad to do in the museum. Suddenly, Katie felt sorry for Mr. Weir. He'd probably never met anyone like George before.

"Can we go to the Hall of Dinosaurs?" Kevin asked. "I used to go there all the time when I was little."

"When was that . . . yesterday?" Suzanne joked.

Kevin stuck his tongue out at her.

"We'll get to the dinosaurs when *I* say so," Mr. Weir said. "We're starting with the ancient Egypt exhibit."

"Do you have any real mummies in there?" George asked excitedly.

Mr. Weir shook his head. "No. Those go to the big museums in the city," he said with a

very jealous sigh. "We get stuck with the fake mummy cases."

"But they look just like the real thing," Mrs. Derkman assured class 3A.

Mr. Weir led them down a long hallway. The walls were lined with drawings made by ancient Egyptians.

"Those are called hieroglyphics," Suzanne told the others. "It's sort of a picture alphabet."

"How did you know that?" Mr. Weir asked, surprised.

"I know a lot about ancient Egypt," Suzanne told him. "I used to be Cleopatra's biggest fan. Until I got tired of her. Then I moved on to Coco Chanel. She was a famous clothing designer. And now I'm interested in learning about supermodels." She turned her face to the side. "Don't you think my bone structure is perfect?"

Mr. Weir glared at Suzanne. "Is there some way to turn her off?" he asked Mrs. Derkman.

Mrs. Derkman sighed. "Suzanne, right now we're talking about ancient Egypt," she said.

Becky Stern had been carefully studying some of the hieroglyphics on the wall. There was one picture that really interested her. It was of a man standing on his head.

Becky flipped over and stood on her hands. "Look at me!" she squealed. "I'm a hieroglyphic."

"Becky!" Katie shouted out, surprised. "Get down. You're going to break something."

"Yes, Becky," Mrs. Derkman scolded. "Get down. We walk on our feet, not our hands, in a museum."

"Katie, you're such a goodie-goodie!" Becky replied. She swung her legs down to the floor.

Unfortunately, Becky didn't see that Manny was standing right behind her. She kicked him in the stomach on her way down. Manny fell backwards and knocked over one of the three fake mummy cases. *Wham!*

Click. Jeremy took a picture of Manny, Becky, and the fallen mummy case. "That's going to be great!" he told Kevin.

Mrs. Derkman glared at Becky and Manny.

"It wasn't my fault," Manny told the teacher.

"You banged into the mummy case," Becky said.

"You banged into *me*," Manny argued.

"I told you this would happen," Katie reminded Becky.

"Be quiet, goodie-goodie," Becky said to Katie. She turned to Manny. "You want to fight about it?"

"I'd never hit a girl," Manny began. "But in your case, I could make an exception."

"Is this the kind of behavior you teach your class?" Mr. Weir asked Mrs. Derkman.

"They're just a little excited, that's all," Mrs. Derkman assured him nervously. She stood between Becky and Manny so they couldn't fight.

Bam! At that very moment, one of the still-standing mummy cases burst open. Something—or someone—leaped out at the class.

"Aaaaahhhh!" Miriam Chan screamed. "It's a mummy!" She headed for the door. As she ran, she stepped right on Mr. Weir's foot.

"Ow!" he shouted, grabbing his foot. "Darn kids!"

Suddenly, they heard some very familiar laughter. It was George. He'd been hiding in the mummy case.

"George, that was mean," Miriam shouted. "You scared me!"

"It was just a joke," George replied.

"Your behavior is not funny!" Mrs. Derkman scolded him.

"You want funny?" George asked her. "I'll give you funny. How do you make a mummy float?"

"How?" Kevin asked.

"Take two scoops of ice cream, add root

beer, then drop in a mummy!"

"George Brennan, get over here right now!" Mrs. Derkman ordered. George walked nervously over to his teacher.

"Apologize to Mr. Weir," the teacher insisted.

"I'm sorry, Mr. Weird," George said.

"It's *Weir*!" Mr. Weir shouted. "And don't you forget it!"

Chapter 4

Mr. Weir led the kids through a large open room. There was no one in there but class 3A. It was very quiet . . . until Mrs. Derkman let out a loud scream. The teacher was standing in the middle of the room, frozen in place.

"What's wrong?" Mr. Weir asked her.

Mrs. Derkman didn't say anything. She just pointed up at a massive plastic spider hanging from the ceiling. Mrs. Derkman was scared of any kind of creepy crawly creature. A giant one like that scared her even more! "W . . . w . . . what's that?" she stammered.

"Oh, that? It's a model of a tarantula," Mr. Weir answered. "Of course, a real tarantula only has a three-and-a-half-inch body and a nine-inch leg span. This is an oversized model. We use it to point out all the interesting parts of a tarantula's body. Notice the spiny hairs that cover its middle section."

Mrs. Derkman kept staring at the giant spider hanging from the ceiling. "I had a nightmare about a tarantula once." Mrs. Derkman gulped. "It didn't end well."

As Mr. Weir talked about the spider, Mandy studied the rows of shelves in the room. They went from the floor to the ceiling. There were lots of fake insects on them.

"I bet I can climb to the top before you do," Mandy dared Jeremy.

"No way," Becky told her. "Jeremy's the best climber in the whole school." She batted her eyes at Jeremy.

Jeremy groaned.

"Come on," Mandy said. "Let's race."

"Okay, you're on!" Jeremy said.

He pulled himself up onto a shelf. Mandy

climbed up behind him.

"Look at us, we're climbing like spiders!" Jeremy called down to Katie.

Mrs. Derkman was too busy staring at the giant tarantula to notice Mandy and Jeremy climbing on the shelves. Mr. Weir was too busy listening to himself talk about spiders to even think about the kids. Mr. Weir liked the sound of his own voice.

"Get down, you guys. Someone could get hurt," Katie warned her friends.

"Katie, stop being a goodie-goodie," Mandy said.

Just then, Mr. Weir spotted Mandy and Jeremy on the shelves. "Get down from there!" he shouted.

"WHOA!!!" Jeremy lost his footing. He fell to the floor with a thud.

That made Mandy fall, too. A whole shelf's worth of plastic moths, caterpillars, flies, and worms tipped over onto her and Jeremy.

Jeremy threw his camera over to Manny.

"Quick! Take this picture," he told Manny.

"Why did I ever get out of bed this morning?" Mr. Weir groaned as the flash went off right in his eyes.

Seeing all those fake bugs on top of her students was worse than any nightmare Mrs. Derkman had ever had. "I was just thinking the same thing," she murmured.

× × ×

The exhibit in the next room was of Native Americans. There was a wooden canoe in the middle of the room. Inside the canoe were four statues of Native Americans. They looked like they were paddling across a river.

"Here are some examples of Native American weaving," Mr. Weir told the class. He pointed to a glass cabinet filled with baskets and rugs.

Katie studied the baskets. They were all very pretty, with interesting patterns woven into the straw. Suddenly, she heard some of the kids behind her laughing hysterically.

Katie turned around to see what was so funny. She couldn't believe her eyes!

George Brennan was sitting in the back of the big canoe! He was pretending to be one of the statues. When George saw the class looking at him, he moved his arms back and forth, like he was paddling the canoe. "Hey, Kevin," George shouted out. "Can you canoe?"

"Sure," Kevin answered. "Canoe? Get it?"

The class laughed even harder. Jeremy took a picture of George paddling in the canoe.

"Mrs. Derkman!" Katie pointed to the

canoe. "Look what George is doing."

The teacher turned around quickly. "George Brennan, you will be up the creek without a paddle if you don't get down from there right now!" Mrs. Derkman ordered sternly.

George had heard Mrs. Derkman sound like that before. He knew she meant business. Quickly, he climbed out of the canoe. Then he strutted proudly over to where Manny and Kevin were standing.

"That was classic, dude!" Manny said, giving George a high five.

Mr. Weir wiped another bead of sweat from off his forehead. "Kids," he muttered angrily under his breath.

✕　✕　✕

After that, George had to walk beside Mrs. Derkman. "Thanks a lot, goodie-goodie," he whispered to Katie as the class entered the mineral and gemstone room.

"It's not my fault," Katie told him. "You were the one who climbed in the canoe."

"But you're the one who told on me," George snapped back.

"Mrs. Derkman would have seen you, anyway. Everyone saw you," Katie told him.

"This room is filled with precious and semiprecious gems. We also have ordinary minerals from all over the world," Mr. Weir told the class.

"Do you have rubies?" Miriam asked him. "That's my birthstone."

"How about diamonds?" Mandy asked.

"I know where you can find the biggest diamonds," George interrupted. "On a baseball field!"

The kids laughed.

Mr. Weir rolled his eyes and looked at his watch.

"Are there any star sapphires in your collection?" Suzanne asked. "I love them. My mother has a dark blue one that she wears on a chain around her neck. My grandmother . . ."

"How about charcoal?" Kevin interrupted.

He made his voice high and squeaky to sound like a girl's. "I adore charcoal. Look at my charcoal ring." He held out his hand to show everyone his imaginary ring.

Some of the boys started to laugh.

"Don't make fun of Suzanne," Katie said, standing up for her best friend.

"Oh, what a goodie-goodie," Kevin told her.

"I am not," Katie insisted.

"If I could actually say something . . ." Mr. Weir began.

But before Mr. Weir could finish his sentence, Manny shouted out from across the room. "Hey, you guys. Check this out!"

Everyone turned around. Manny was sitting on top of a huge slab of polished jade.

"Get down from there!" Mr. Weir shouted.

"Okay," Manny agreed. "Wheeeeeeeeee!" He slid down the slab of jade like it was the slide in the playground.

Mr. Weir took out a handkerchief and wiped the back of his neck. "Is it getting warm in here?" he asked nervously.

"Perhaps we should try the North American Wildlife room," Mrs. Derkman suggested. She began to lead the class away from the rock and mineral room.

"I'm so mad at Manny," Miriam moaned as the class left the mineral and gemstone room. "I wanted to see a real ruby."

Katie frowned. "You were right, Suzanne," she said. "Boys can be real pains. I can't believe Manny did that."

Suzanne shrugged. "Actually, I thought he was pretty funny. But I can see why you'd be upset by it, seeing as you're a goodie-goodie and all."

Chapter 5

Suzanne's comment upset Katie. But she was even more upset about what was in the North American Wildlife room. There, the kids came face to face with bears, mountain lions, and buffalo. Unfortunately, all of the animals were dead and stuffed. They were part of giant dioramas. And, unlike the mummies, these were all real. Or, at least, they once were!

That made Katie very sad. She loved animals. She had a cocker spaniel, Pepper, who she'd raised ever since he was a pup. Katie and Pepper were always together—except when she was in school or at the mall. Dogs weren't allowed there.

Katie was also a vegetarian. She would never eat anything that had once had a face. Now, here she was in a room full of animals that had been hunted and put on display. It was awful!

Suzanne noticed that Katie was upset. "You should just walk right out of here," she told her. "It could be your way of protesting the killing of innocent animals."

Kevin overheard Suzanne. "Katie couldn't do that," he said. "She's too much of a goodie-goodie to break the rules."

Suzanne nodded. "You're right," she agreed. Then she turned to Katie. "Maybe you should just close your eyes until we leave."

Katie wasn't sure what made her angrier— the dead animals or the way her friends were teasing her about being a goodie-goodie. She had to do something. *But what?*

The class stopped in front of a stuffed brown bear. Mr. Weir began to speak. "This is the grizzly bear. It lives . . ."

Suddenly, the bear seemed to speak. "Let me out!"

Mr. Weir jumped back. "Who said that?" he demanded.

"Animals have feelings!" the bear bellowed angrily. "How would you like to be stuffed and put in here? *ROAR!*"

Just then, a little girl looking up at the bear burst into tears. "Mommy, that bear roared at me!" she cried.

The girl wasn't the only toddler in the room. Once she started crying, a pair of twin boys in a double stroller joined in. "No like bears!" one of them sobbed.

"Me, neither," cried his brother.

"WAAAAHHHHH!" The girl was really wailing now.

The sound of the shrieking toddlers really upset Mr. Weir. With each cry, his face turned redder and redder. More sweat built up on his forehead. A thick blue vein popped out on his neck.

Flash! Jeremy took a picture of Mr. Weir. "That one's a classic!" he laughed.

Mr. Weir glared at Jeremy. Then he eyed the rest of the kids in class 3A suspiciously. "Which of you *wild animals* made that bear speak?" he demanded.

George burst out laughing. "Good one, Katie Kazoo!" he cheered.

Everyone turned toward Katie. She smiled proudly.

"Katie, was that you?" Mrs. Derkman asked, surprised.

"Sure it was," George said. "She was using ventriloquism to make the bear talk. Katie's great at ventriloquism. She doesn't move her lips one bit." He turned to Manny. "Remember the time she made your backpack talk? Boy, were you freaked out!"

Manny blushed.

"I guess you're not a goodie-goodie, after all," George told Katie.

Katie smiled. Coming from George, that

was a big compliment.

"*Roar!*" Katie made the bear say.

"WAAAAHHHH!" cried the two-year-old girl.

"EEEYAAHHH!" screamed the twins.

Mr. Weir stuck his fingers in his ears to block out the noise.

"That's it!" he shouted angrily. "Young lady, leave this room right now."

"But, Mr. Weir," Mrs. Derkman interrupted. "I don't want to send one of my students off on her own in the museum."

"She'll be fine," Mr. Weir assured the teacher. "There are plenty of guards around. Any one of them can help her if she's got a problem."

"But . . ." Mrs. Derkman began.

"If she doesn't leave, I won't continue this tour," Mr. Weir said. "I'm tired of dealing with your students. They're acting like children."

"They *are* children," Mrs. Derkman reminded him.

"Either she leaves, or I do," Mr. Weir said angrily.

Mrs. Derkman sighed. "Katie, there's a library right down the hall. Instead of looking at the bears, you can do a small report on grizzlies. I'm sure the librarian can help you find information."

The kids all felt bad for Katie. An extra report. That really stunk!

Katie was a little sad that she would be missing the rest of the field trip. And she felt bad about scaring the little kids. But she was also proud of herself. She'd let everyone know that she thought killing animals was wrong. And she'd proved to her friends that she wasn't a goodie-goodie.

A report was a small price to pay for all that.

Chapter 6

Katie went out into the hall. She looked for a guard who could show her where the library was. But there was no one in the hallway.

Suddenly, she felt a small draft on the back of her neck. That was weird. There were no windows anywhere near her.

The draft became a breeze. Then the breeze grew stronger. Katie looked for an open window. All of the windows were shut. The breeze couldn't be coming from there, either.

Katie gulped. This wasn't any ordinary wind. This was the magic wind!

Whoosh! The magic wind picked up speed. It swirled wildly around Katie. She shut her eyes tightly and tried not to cry. The wind was big, powerful, and out of control. Katie was really scared!

But she was even more scared when the wind *stopped* blowing. She knew what that meant. The magic wind was gone . . .

And so was Katie Carew.

Chapter 7

Katie slowly opened her eyes and looked around. She wasn't in the hall anymore. The magic wind had blown her into the Hall of Dinosaurs. Everywhere Katie looked, she saw huge, prehistoric skeletons.

Okay, so now she knew where she was. But she still didn't know *who* she was.

Mandy looked up at Katie. "Was the Stegosaurus a plant-eater or a meat-eater?" she asked.

"Huh?" Katie replied.

"What did the Stegosaurus eat?" Mandy asked again.

"Um . . . let me think about that for a moment," Katie answered.

"But you're the Director of the Education Department. You should know all about this," Mandy said disappointedly.

"Stegosaurus was a plant-eater," Mrs. Derkman told her.

Katie didn't hear Mrs. Derkman's answer. She was too busy thinking about what Mandy had called her. *The Director of the Education Department?* Katie gulped. That was Mr. Weir's title!

Katie looked down at her feet. Her purple sneakers were gone. In their place was a pair of worn, black loafers. She was also wearing gray slacks and a white sweat-stained, button-down shirt. There was a badge on a chain around her neck. Katie looked at the picture on the badge. It showed a skinny man with a tuft of hair on the top of his head.

Oh, no!

The magic wind had turned Katie into Mr. Weir!

"What kind of dinosaur is this?" Manny

43

asked her. He was standing beside a huge, long-necked dinosaur skeleton.

Katie didn't answer. She was too busy staring at the picture on her badge. Katie felt like she was going to cry. She didn't want to be Mr. Weir. Not for one minute.

"Whoa, look at this tooth," Jeremy called out from the other side of the room. He pointed to a huge, pointy fossil. "It's as sharp as a knife."

"I wouldn't want to be his dentist," Kevin said.

"That belonged to an Allosaurus," Mrs. Derkman told the boys. "They were meat-eaters." She turned to Katie. "Mr. Weir, I think maybe there are too many children here for you. It will be easier for you to answer questions from just a few."

"Huh?" Katie murmured. She hadn't been listening to Mrs. Derkman at all.

"Sometimes, it's difficult for people who aren't teachers to handle large groups of third-graders," Mrs. Derkman replied. "So I'm going to take some of these children into the next room. You can handle the others."

"No!" Katie shouted without thinking. She didn't want to be in charge.

"Excuse me?" Mrs. Derkman said.

Katie sighed. She had forgotten she was supposed to be Mr. Weir. "I mean, no problem," she corrected herself.

Mrs. Derkman took Jeremy, Becky, Zoe, and Manny into the next room. Everyone else stayed with Katie.

"Man, I can't believe we got stuck with Mr. Weird," Kevin whispered to Suzanne. "He hates kids."

"Would you rather be with Mrs. Derkman?" Suzanne asked him.

Kevin sighed. "I'd rather be out on the playground," he said.

Suzanne turned to Katie. "Mr. Weir," she said. "I heard the dinosaurs were all beautiful colors, like birds. Is that true?"

Katie had no idea. So she gave a Mr. Weir kind of answer. "How should I know? I'm not old enough to have been around in the time of the dinosaurs."

"I was just asking," Suzanne muttered.

"Oh, look at this one," Miriam pointed to a nest with a few eggs and some smaller dinosaur skeletons in it. "It's a baby. What kind of dinosaur is this, Mr. Weir?"

"Not a very smart one," Katie said.

"Huh?" Miriam asked.

"Any dinosaur that would have children would have to be foolish," Katie explained.

"Oh, man, this stinks!" Kevin moaned as he read one of the signs.

"What does?" Suzanne asked him.

Kevin pointed to a sign next to one of the smaller dinosaurs. "It says here that none of the dinosaur skeletons in this room are real. They're just models."

"The real dinosaurs are probably in museums in the big cities," Suzanne told him.

"Just like the real mummies. Isn't that right, Mr. Weir?"

Before Katie could answer, a loud shout came from the other side of the room.

"Yeehah! Ride 'em, cowboy!" someone yelled.

Katie turned around just in time to see George sitting on the back of a model of a huge meat-eating dinosaur!

"How did you get up there?" Kevin asked, impressed.

"I climbed up the tail," George answered. He pointed to the trail of bones that led from the floor, straight up to the dinosaur's head. "See, it's like a ladder."

"Cool. I want to try it next," Kevin said.

This was getting out of hand. Katie couldn't let the boys climb up and down on the dinosaurs. "George, get down from there right now!" she demanded.

"No way, Mr. Weird," George answered. "A cowboy doesn't get down till he's thrown from the horse. Yeehah!" He pretended to swing an imaginary lasso.

"Please get down," Katie tried again. "You're going to get in trouble."

"That won't scare George," Suzanne told her. "He's always in trouble."

Katie reached up and tried to grab George. But George was quicker—he leaped from the dinosaur's back onto the floor. Then he ran off.

"George! Get back here!" Katie ordered. But George just kept on running. Katie followed him. Suzanne, Kevin, Mandy, and Miriam ran after Katie.

George darted into a large room. The sign on the door read "Not Open to the Public." But George didn't take the time to read the sign. He just ran right in.

Inside the room were two dinosaur models and all sorts of tools. This was the room where the museum's scientists put together the model dinosaurs. But the scientists weren't in there right now.

Unfortunately, George was.

"George! Get out!" Katie shouted as she followed him into the room.

Quickly, George climbed up the long tail of one of the dinosaurs. He sat on the dinosaur's big head and stuck his tongue out.

That made Katie mad. She started to climb up the dinosaur's tail after George. But the fake bones couldn't hold the weight of a grown man. And that's just what Katie was at the moment . . .

CRASH!

Chapter 8

The dinosaur's tailbones collapsed to the floor like giant prehistoric dominoes. In seconds, Katie and George were sitting on the ground, surrounded by a pile of white plastic bones and wire.

"Oops," George said sheepishly.

"Oops?" Katie cried out. "Is that all you can say? Look what you've done!"

"I didn't do it. You did," George said. He rubbed his bottom. "And how come you only care about the dinosaur? I hurt my tail, too."

Katie didn't care about George's sore rear end. All she could think about was the pile of bones on the floor. Mr. Weir was going to be in

big trouble. He might even lose his job! And it would all be Katie's fault.

A tear ran down Katie's cheek.

"Whoa, check it out," Kevin said. "Mr. Weird is crying."

Katie gulped. She didn't know a lot about being the Director of the Education Department. But she was pretty sure that someone like Mr. Weir did not cry. At least, not in front of kids. Quickly, she used the sleeve of Mr. Weir's shirt to dry her eyes. "I am not crying," she corrected Kevin. "My eyeballs are just sweating."

"I've never heard of sweating eyeballs," Kevin told her.

"I believe his eyeballs are sweating. Every other part of him is sweating," Suzanne noted.

It was true. Mr. Weir's shirt was covered with perspiration. Katie felt dampness on the back of her neck and on her forehead, too. Her underarms were disgusting. Yuck. Katie frowned. Being Mr. Weir really stunk . . . in more ways than one.

Katie didn't like Mr. Weir at all. But she didn't want him to lose his job. There was only one thing to do. "We've got to put this dinosaur's tail back together," she told the kids.

"Us?" Kevin asked. "We don't know anything about being palea . . . paleee . . . pileontol . . ."

"You mean paleontologists," Mandy told him. "Dinosaur scientists."

Kevin nodded. "See, I can't even pronounce it," he told Katie. "How am I supposed to be one?"

Katie sighed. Kevin was right. They didn't know anything about being paleontologists. But they couldn't just leave that pile of bones sitting there. They had to at least try to put the dinosaur's tail back together. "How hard can it be?" Katie asked the kids.

"Really hard," Kevin answered.

"You played with blocks when you were little, didn't you? This can't be much different. All we have to do is follow this picture." Katie pointed to a drawing of the completed dinosaur skeleton.

George picked up one of the bones. "This looks like the bottom of the tail," he said quietly.

Katie smiled at him. She could tell he was sorry for what had happened. None of his pranks had ever turned out this badly before. Maybe George would be a little more of a goodie-goodie himself after this.

"Okay," she told him. "Let's get started."

Kevin picked up a big bone. "Good thing Katie's dog's not here," he said. "Can you imagine how he'd love these things? They're huge."

"Pepper would have a lot of fun here," Katie agreed.

"Hey," Suzanne asked. "How'd you know her dog is named Pepper?"

Katie gulped. She'd forgotten she was supposed to be Mr. Weir! "I didn't," she said quickly. "I . . . uh . . . I was talking about my dog. *His* name is Pepper."

"Poor Katie," Suzanne whispered to Miriam. "First, Mrs. Derkman moves in next door to her. Now, Mr. Weir's dog has the same name as hers. Good thing she's not here to find out about that!"

Katie sighed. That was a close one.

"I'm getting hungry," George moaned.

"You're always hungry," Suzanne told him.

"Lunch isn't for another fifteen minutes," Kevin moaned as he looked at the clock on the wall.

Katie gulped. Fifteen minutes? That was hardly any time at all. They had to get the dinosaur's tail fixed before Mrs. Derkman came back. They would all be in big trouble if she found out what had happened.

"Faster, faster," Katie urged the kids. "We've got to get this thing together."

"We're almost done, Mr. Weir," Mandy said. "There's just this one big bone left."

Katie took the bone from Mandy. Quickly, she used it to attach the dinosaur to its tail. "Finished," she said, taking a deep breath.

"It looks pretty good," Kevin said. "Almost like the real thing."

"Almost?" Katie asked nervously.

"It's not like the picture," Kevin told her.

Katie looked at the picture. Oh, no! Kevin was right. In the picture, the dinosaur's tail was pointing down to the ground. Now, its tail was pointing straight out.

"Maybe no one will notice," George suggested.

"Are you kidding?" Kevin asked. "Who could miss that?"

Beep. Beep. Beep. Before Katie could say anything, she heard a strange noise coming from her shirt pocket.

Startled, Katie looked down. She reached into her pocket and pulled out a small, black pager. She looked at the words on the screen.

COME TO YOUR OFFICE. DR. MUFFINSTOFFER HAS ARRIVED.

Katie gulped. Dr. Muffinstoffer was the famous scientist Mr. Weir was supposed to meet with. Now, Katie was going to have to be the one to show him around the museum.

But Katie didn't know anything about the museum!

This was so not good.

Chapter 9

"Um, I have to go," Katie nervously told the kids.

"You can't just leave us here," Suzanne said.

"I'll be right back," Katie said as she raced into the hall. "Don't move until I get here. And, whatever you do, *don't touch that dinosaur!*"

Katie had no idea where Mr. Weir's office could be. For a moment, she thought about asking one of the guards how to get there. But she looked like Mr. Weir now. Mr. Weir would surely know the way to his own office. If she asked for directions, the guard would surely think that Mr. Weir *was* weird.

Katie wandered around the museum until

she came to what seemed to be a row of offices. Maybe this was where Mr. Weir worked. Quickly, Katie opened the first office door and stepped inside.

Oops. This was definitely not Mr. Weir's office. Instead of a desk and books, the room was filled with mops, pails, and cleaning supplies. Katie was in the janitor's closet!

She reached for the doorknob. But before she could open the door, Katie felt a cool breeze blowing on the back of her neck. There were no windows in the closet and the door was shut tightly. Katie knew right away that this was no ordinary wind. This was the magic wind.

The magic wind grew stronger and stronger. It whirled around Katie like a tornado. Faster and faster it blew, until the wind was so strong that Katie could barely breathe.

And then it stopped. Just like that. The magic wind was gone.

Slowly, Katie opened her eyes and looked down at her feet. Her purple sneakers were back. So were her jeans. And there wasn't even a trace of sweat on her tank top.

She was Katie Carew again!

Katie knew she should find her way to the library and wait for her class. But Katie wanted to be with the rest of her class in the Hall of Dinosaurs. Unfortunately, she had no idea how to get back there.

But the real Mr. Weir certainly did.

As Katie stepped out into the hall, she found him standing outside an office door. He was staring at his beeper.

"Mr. Weir," Katie said. "What are you doing here?"

"I don't know," he mumbled. "One minute, I was in the Hall of Dinosaurs and the next thing I knew, I was standing outside of my office." He stared at Katie for a moment. "What are you doing here?"

"Um, I came to get you," Katie said quickly.

Mr. Weir didn't ask her why. He just kept staring at his beeper. "Dr. Muffinstoffer is supposed to be in my office. But I don't remember hearing my beeper or walking over here. And Dr. Muffinstoffer isn't here."

Katie didn't know what to say. She wasn't sure why Dr. Muffinstoffer had disappeared. She just hoped that it wasn't her fault. Too many things had been her fault today.

"How about we go back to the dinosaurs?" Katie said quickly.

Mr. Weir sighed. "I've got to get a new job," he moaned. "This one is too stressful."

Chapter 10

When Mr. Weir and Katie arrived in the Hall of Dinosaurs, only the kids who had been with Mrs. Derkman were there. The teacher looked frantic.

"Mr. Weir!" she cried out. "Where have you been? And where are my students?"

"I . . . um . . . er . . . I'm not certain," Mr. Weir mumbled.

Mrs. Derkman gasped. "You lost my students?"

"Well, not exactly," Mr. Weir said. "I'm sure they're around here somewhere."

"I know where they are," Katie interrupted. "Follow me."

Katie led her teacher and Mr. Weir to the back hallway and into the room where the dinosaur models were built. Sure enough, the kids were all there. So was a small man with a long white beard and glasses.

"Dr. Muffinstoffer, I can explain," Mr. Weir said as he walked over to the man with the beard. "At least I think I can . . . I'm not really sure."

"It's fine. When you weren't in your office, I started to walk around the museum myself," the famous scientist explained.

"I don't know why I wasn't there," Mr. Weir apologized. "I don't know anything."

"You can sure say that again," Jeremy whispered to George.

"Fascinating," Dr. Muffinstoffer muttered. He was looking at the tail on the dinosaur model. "I don't know how you did this."

"I'm not sure, either. It's all kind of fuzzy," Mr. Weir sighed.

"There are only a few paleontologists in

the world who are aware of the change," Dr. Muffinstoffer continued.

"The change?" Kevin asked.

"Yes." Dr. Muffinstoffer pointed to the dinosaur's tail. "This dinosaur was always thought to walk with its tail upright. Recently, we figured out that the tail stuck straight out, just like you have it here. The tail helped it balance." He turned to Mr. Weir. "But that information hasn't even been published yet. How did you know about it?"

"Well . . . I . . . I mean . . . er . . ." Mr. Weir stammered. He didn't know what to say.

"Mr. Weir knows all the up-to-date information. He rebuilt the tail himself," Katie butted in. "Some of the kids in our class helped."

"What an interesting project," Dr. Muffinstoffer said with a smile.

"There's no better way to learn about dinosaurs than to help build one, is there Mr. Weir?" Katie said.

"I, um . . . er . . . sure. I guess," Mr. Weir said. He was staring at the tail on the model dinosaur.

Jeremy pulled out his camera. "I want to get a picture of you guys with the dinosaur," he said to Mandy, Miriam, Kevin, Suzanne, and George. He turned to Dr. Muffinstoffer and Mr. Weir. "Would you be in it, too?"

"Now why would I want to . . ." Mr. Weir began angrily.

"It would be my absolute pleasure," Dr. Muffinstoffer interrupted.

"Exactly what I was going to say," Mr. Weir quickly added.

Katie choked back a laugh. That wasn't at all what Mr. Weir was going to say. He was just trying to impress Dr. Muffinstoffer.

Suzanne, George, Kevin, Mandy, and Miriam all gathered for their picture. Mr. Weir fluffed the tuft of hair on the top of his head and fixed the collar of his sweaty shirt. He wanted to be sure he looked good.

"You must really like children," Dr. Muffinstoffer said as he stood next to Mr. Weir.

"Oh, I love them," Mr. Weir said. "Ask anyone."

George was about to open his mouth to disagree, but he shut it quickly. He'd caused enough trouble for one day.

"Okay, everyone," Jeremy said. "Say dinosaur."

"Dinosaur!"

CHERRYDALE SCH

Chapter 11

"Wow! You guys were so lucky to be in Mr. Weir's group," Jeremy told George and Suzanne as he got onto the school bus behind them. "You got to *build* a dinosaur. We had to listen to Mrs. Derkman talk about them."

"We did have a lot of fun," Suzanne admitted. "Even if we were with Mr. Weird. It was a nice way to spend our last third-grade field trip."

"Yeah," Mandy chimed in. "It's hard to believe that this school year is almost over. Summer's almost here."

"My big brother Ian says fourth grade is very different than third," Kevin said nervously. "It's a lot harder."

"Different's okay," George said. "We'll have new teachers." He didn't sound upset about that at all.

"But we won't be together," Becky Stern told the others. "There are two fourth-grade classes. Some of us will be in one class, and some will be in the other." She looked at Jeremy and sighed. She didn't want to be in a different class than him.

Jeremy rolled his eyes. *He* wouldn't mind it if he and Becky were in a different class next year.

"We can all play together at recess and after school," Katie said, trying to be cheerful. "We'll still be friends."

"Yeah, but it won't be the same," Mandy told her.

"I guess we're in for a lot of changes," Suzanne shrugged.

Just then, Katie felt a cool breeze blowing on the back of her neck. She gasped. Was it possible that the magic wind had come to change her into someone else?

The magic wind wouldn't do that in front of other people. Or would it? Katie didn't know for sure. It was hard to say what the magic wind would or wouldn't do. She closed her eyes and got ready for the tornado to start swirling around her.

"George, close that window!" Suzanne shouted out suddenly. "The wind is ruining my hair."

Katie breathed a sigh of relief. It wasn't the magic wind, after all. It was just the breeze from an open window. "Don't worry, George, I'll close it," Katie replied.

"Ow!" Suzanne groaned. "George, stop pulling on my ponytail!"

"It wasn't me," George said. "I think it was Jeremy."

"Not me." Jeremy shook his head. "Maybe it was Manny."

Suzanne frowned and folded her arms

across her chest. "I hate boys," she sighed.

Katie laughed. Some things never changed.

Class 3A's Dino Fun Facts

Class 3A learned a lot about dinosaurs at the museum. (Most of all, they learned never to climb on top of one!) Here are some of the fun facts they gathered on their field trip:

✕ Dinosaurs lived everywhere! Their bones have been found all over the Earth—even in the Arctic Circle and near the South Pole.

✕ The biggest known dinosaurs were the plant-eating Argentinosaurus huinculensis. They grew to be 115–130 feet long. They had long necks that allowed them to reach the leaves in tall trees. They also had huge tails that helped them keep their balance.

✕ It is harder to find small dinosaur fossils than large ones. So far, the smallest known dinosaur is the Microraptor. It was only about sixteen inches long, which makes it no bigger than a crow. It was discovered in China.

✕ The Diplodocus was the dinosaur with the longest tail. Its tail could grow to about forty-three feet long!

✕ The deadliest dinosaurs were fast, bird-like meat-eaters. These Megaraptor, Utahraptor, and Deinonychus dinosaurs all had huge claws, sharp teeth, and wing-like arms that helped them move quickly during a chase.

✕ The plant-eating Hadrosaurs had 960 teeth! (How'd you like to have to brush all of those?)